What's the Time?

Tony Bradman

Illustrated by Priscilla Lamont

What's the time?

It’s time to begin.
It’s time to listen,

and then join in.

What's the time?
It's time to draw.

It's time to read,
and read some more.

What's the time?
It's time to eat,

it’s time to drink,

and leave things neat.

What's the time?
It's time to play.

It's time to add and
take away.

What's the time?
Now don't you know?

It's time to get your coat . . .

. . . and go!